Bullet Points
Volume 7

Bullet Points
Volume 7

Nathan W. Toronto

Editor

Bullet Point Press

Paperback edition, first impression, October 2024
ISBN 979-8-2241216-0-1

The Arabic block *noon* colophon is a trademark of BULLET POINT PRESS.

Cover design by Nathan W. Toronto. Cover © 2024 Nathan W. Toronto. Cover image by Maksim Shmeljov (used under license). Interior design by Nathan W. Toronto using the Spectral LaTeX font.

Other editions: ISBN 979-8-3414865-2-2 (paperback) | ISBN 979-8-2275726-0-8 (electronic) | ASIN B0DJMGR18X (electronic)

For those who fight for their friends.

Typset using LaTeX.

Why We Fight

THE STORIES IN THIS VOLUME of *Bullet Points* explore combat motivation. It is impossible to say how anyone will react to the horrors of combat before they are faced with it. A trove of research has explored this question, identifying patriotism, a desire for money, the threat of discipline, and even sadism as key motivators in combat. However, since the publication of Allan R. Millet and Williamson Murray's seminal three-volume work, *Military Effectiveness*, the conventional wisdom has suggested that love for comrades is the strongest motivator in combat.

Each story in this volume explores some aspect of love as combat motivation. In "We Held Hands, We Held Fire," Myna Chang shows what happens at the moment of destruction. In "Witness for the Dead," Addison Smith describes in vivid detail the atoning love of a mother for a child. Adam Gaffen's "Lupus in Astris" explores the interplay between a fellow warrior's need and managing post-combat stress. The main character's concern for others in Dawn Vogel's "Child's Play" teaches us a great deal about how and why we fight. In "Cold Cowardice," Wesley Zurovec shows the agonizing tension between regard for those we fight beside and concern for those left on the home front. Kevin Brown, in "The Final Float," shows how formative experiences with a friend can change our will to fight. Finally, in "Loyalty," Anatoly Belilovsky explores how combat motivation even impacts how we treat an enemy.

Military science fiction gives insights into the combat experience that reams of research into the subject cannot. The explorations in this volume are visceral and human, not antiseptic and scientific. Combat is not a lab experiment, but a chaotic and horrible human endeavor, and we are well-served to reflect on it through fiction.

—Nathan W. Toronto, ed.

CONTENTS

We Held Hands, We Held Fire

Myna Chang

Myna Chang (she/her) is the host of *Electric Sheep SF* and publisher of *MicroVerse Recommended Reading*. Her work has been selected for *Locus Recommended Reading List*, *Norton's Flash Fiction America*, *Best Small Fictions*, and *Best Microfiction*. See more at MynaChang.com or find her on Bluesky or X @MynaChang.

THE RESCUE SHIP FELL out of orbit, sparking firefly phosphorescence as the engines ignited celestial gas. We huddled by the watchtower, unbreathing as the ship broke apart. It carved boiled-orange trails under the edge of our heaven, rescuers turned supersonic projectiles, evac troops showering Titan like mythical rain. The scientists abandoned us, retreating to the habitat bubble, hoping the welds would hold, the code wouldn't scramble. In those fiery moments, we discovered touch. Engineered skin on skin, we held hands, grasped the forbidden frisson of shared heat, mingled DNA. Almost-human comfort. Fingers entwined, we faced cataclysm—and drank burning sky.

Witness for the Dead

ADDISON SMITH

Addison Smith (he/him) has blood made of cold brew and flesh made of chocolate. His fiction has appeared in *Fantasy Magazine*, *Escape Pod*, and *Daily Science Fiction*, among others. Addison is a member of the Codex Writers Group and you can find him on Bluesky @addisoncs.bsky.social.

THE WOMAN LAY PRONE with a child in her arms, huddled around her like it was her sworn duty to protect. Needlepoint marks dotted the skin across her body and bled lines around her arms and thighs, striping her figure in red. Snow packed red around her body. Jason flipped his helmet up and stared. Behind him, his soldiers looked away and searched the rest of the shelter.

The crawlers stood feet away, deactivated and terrifying. Years of fighting had led to the attack, the incursion, and the blown EMP that shut them all down in this tiny area of the global battlefield. The crawlers were tiny things, but he had seen what they could do to a human. He saw it now, even as he refused to look at her face or her chest, where most of the damage had been focused. It dug into her, as if desperate to kill everything she meant to protect.

Jason collected himself. It didn't take long, and he hated that new skill. "We've got more," he said into his comm. "Too late."

A sigh came through his comm. No words were necessary. They had all seen their share of bodies. He wondered what it would be like to be his superior, seeing the bodies herself as they scouted the damned city and receiving every notification of bodies found. Had she received a single report of survivors?

Blood dried and froze on the woman's skin, shining red beneath his flashlight. He stared at the crawlers feet away. They had only just left her when the EMP hit. They destroyed her and left to find their next victim. If their attack had been a minute quicker, or had one less hesitation, the two might be alive right now. They would have flagged them down in the streets or hugged him when he came to search for survivors.

Jason's comm crackled. "Verify. How many?"

Jason cursed, comm not yet activated. The huddled child was so small, a skinny frame in the woman's arms. He'd seen enough nightmares. He would see more tonight. He was the witness for the dead and the last who would know them before the city was abandoned to dust and snow.

Jason leaned down and took the woman's arm. Her body was still warm and pliant beneath his gloves hands. He pushed her arm to the side.

A hand shot up, gripping the arm and pulling it back. The child covered herself and quivered beneath the harsh flashlight. Jason stepped back. He stared at the crawlers, deactivated and silent. They stood on sharp and spindly legs, bodies turned not away but toward the girl. Tears welled in his eyes. They weren't leaving when the EMP blew. He listened to the girl's tiny breath, impossible to hide from the machines. They heard her. They were coming back.

Jason sat on the floor of the destroyed building, white light shining through broken windows. He didn't free the girl from her gruesome protection, a body still warm and saving her in death. The girl looked out from beneath the woman's body. Jason removed his armor piece by piece and laid it on the floor before him. When the metal and Kevlar were stripped away, he sat cross-legged and facing the girl. She watched with interest and fear.

"My name is Jason," he said. "I'm here to help you."

The girl watched, wet and matted hair emerging from the body of her protector. She stood, tiny in the giant room, hand clutching dead fingers. She didn't cry. She was in shock. She held something small against her chest, something rectangular in a cloth bundle. She clutched it as if it were the most important thing. "It's going to be okay," Jason said. He reached out a hand, now bare and chill. The girl took his hands and stepped away from the body, limp fingers falling from her grasp.

"What do you have there?" Jason said.

The girl stuttered, her voice small and cracking. "Mommy said it was important. She said it was my mission." She handed the object over and looked around the room. All around soldiers stirred and stared, smiles growing at any sign of life.

Jason unwrapped the object. It was a normal data drive, shielded from the eyes of the enemy. Across its case a message was scrawled in black marker. "Global Network Access Codes. We Fight."

Jason grinned, tears falling from his eyes. It was the most important thing he had ever held. He wrapped his arms around the girl and held her tight. The data became the second most important.

"Are we going to win?" the girl asked.

Jason smiled through tears and held her close. "Yeah," he said. "We're going to win."

Lupus in Astris

Adam Gaffen

Adam Gaffen is the author of the near-future, hopepunk science fiction universe that starts with *The Cassidy Chronicles*. He's also venturing into fantasy and romance with the *Godsfall* trilogy, and into heist novels with *The Vault & the Vixen*, all of which inhabit the Cassidyverse. He's been honored with awards from Writers of the Future, Colorado Authors League, the Go Indie Now network, AllAuthor, Read Free.ly, and the Drunken Druid. He lives in Colorado with his wife, five dogs, and five cats, and wonders where all the time goes.

SHI CRASHED THROUGH THE CORRIDORS of the *Young*, the wolf following her. Its claws scrabbled for purchase on the duralloy deck, steadily catching up to her. She hurled herself around a corner, through the failing lights, running for the bridge, her Captain, and her lover. They'd save her.

There! The final hatch was ahead. Shi skidded to a halt, the pursuing wolf forgotten, as she looked in on the devastated command deck. The vacuum of space reached its greedy fingers toward her. She stiffened and held, the rushing atmosphere carrying the wolf's rank musk.

"No!" she shouted, seeing Icy frozen to her console.

The wolf was close, close enough she could feel the warmth of its breath behind her . . .

Shi jerked upright, sweat pouring from her body, eyes wide and unseeing, and screamed.

"Lieutenant Hendrickson?" The voice of the AI was calm, and the vision of the snarling beast faded into the recesses of her mind.

"Lieutenant Hendrickson?" Hermes asked again.

"I'm here," Shi answered, voice breathy.

"Your appointment is in a half-hour, Lieutenant."

"Thank you." Shi dropped her head into her hands and sat until her breathing eased. Then she stood and prepared for the hardest part of her week.

COMMANDER GENESIS BECKMAN sighed.

"Lieutenant, therapy only works if you talk to me," she said.

Shi didn't answer.

After a few minutes, Beckman said, "Time's up. Thank you for coming, Shi. I look forward to our sessions. They're the most peaceful part of my week."

Shi's head snapped up, but Beckman returned her glare dispassionately. "Problem, Lieutenant?"

Shi mumbled something and stood.

"Same time next week." Beckman returned her attention to work.

WHY DOES EVERYONE WANT me to talk? Shi wondered as she meandered back to the bridge. *For four years I've talked about it! I don't want to talk about it anymore. I just want the nightmares to end.*

She hadn't, of course. She'd told the bare minimum to anyone who'd asked until they stopped asking. The details she kept.

The screams of her crewmates echoed in her mind. Captain Gonzalez, cut in half by a beam slicing through the bridge, dying with her last order unspoken. Weatherby, flung into the ceiling by an uncontrolled spin, her helmet smashed, suffocating in vacuum.

The others were worse. The engineering crew stayed on post, decimated by multiple blasts that blew out the bulkheads and ruptured the conduits. They kept the *Young* in the fight until there was no more to give, until they were all dead.

And Icy. An electrical discharge fused her to the console, even as she tried desperately to save the ship.

Icy's loss cut the deepest.

And then there was Shi. Her console had blown, too, but she'd only caught a fraction of the blast. Enough to knock her out as the dying volley from the *Young* blew the *Anders* into fragments. Enough to keep her alive as the rest of her crew, every man and woman, died.

Her wandering feet led her to the bridge, and Shi tried to lose herself in the work of navigating the *Pike*.

SHI COULD HEAR the wolf. How?

Vacuum surrounded her.

She saw the stars through the hull.

She shouldn't hear anything, but she could. The heavy panting, the rasp of claws, and she knew it was gaining.

Shi rounded the last bend. The bulkhead should be right ahead, but it was gone, vaporized. The stars shone brightly instead.

Maybe she could reach one star. Any star would do. They couldn't be that far anymore.

They'd been out here for, well, she didn't know how long.

She ought to know how long, shouldn't she? Wasn't she the navigator?

A whiff of fetid breath caressed her nostrils. Shi heard an anticipatory growl and scrambled a little harder. The blown-out bulkhead was almost within reach. If she could make it, she'd be safe. The wolf couldn't follow her into the stars.

The heat-warped deck reached and snagged her foot, and she sprawled. Shi fell hard, her breath blown out of her. Then the wolf was upon her, pinning her down. She writhed under its weight, trying to escape, trying to break free . . .

Shi jerked upright, sweat pouring from her body, eyes wide and unseeing, and screamed.

METEOROIDS WERE UBIQUITOUS in most star systems. As a rule of thumb, the younger the system, the more debris would be present, and 497 SSDi Aleph was only two billion years old. A veritable infant, and that meant lots of junk.

The gravitational dynamics made Aleph tricky. Warp drives worked within a star's gravitational well. They even worked in binary or trinary systems, but required finicky, precise calculations.

The problems increased geometrically when the stars were closer together. In Aleph, the locked pair orbited the primary at about four light hours, twenty-nine Astronimical Units, or the distance from the Sun to Neptune.

Gravity was folded, spindled, and mutilated.

Thus, Captain Kassidy Yager wasn't about to warp into the system. Sublight engines would get the *Pike* there, but even the most formidable shields and armoring had limits. Running into a rock a dozen meters across at a substantial fraction of c would ruin everyone's day. Yager considered hanging back and letting the Direwolves run the gauntlet, but they didn't have the proper sensors or equipment. No, if they were going to do a survey, the *Pike* needed to get down and dirty.

"I'm sorry, Captain, I don't understand." Shi stood at attention.

Sitting behind her desk, Captain Yager cocked her head to the side.

"It's a simple concept, Lieutenant. I gave you an order, and you say, 'Yes, ma'am,' and go do it. Unless you can't do it?"

"No, ma'am, I can do it. I just—I just don't understand. Why do you need me on the mission?"

"Ah." Yager smiled. "Sorry, Shi. I'm still learning how to be the Old Woman."

Hendrickson returned the smile with a feeling of surprise.

"The Wolf shuttle pilots are great at judging whether a space is adequate for their ship, down to the decimeter, but they're not great about going larger or less maneuverable. God, I just thought of something horrible."

Shi waited for Yager to continue.

"Imagine if we had to use the Direwolf fighters? Those hotshots would try to sneak through a five-meter gap!" She shook her head, half in amazement and half in disbelief. "Getting back to the point. If I'm going to bring the *Pike* into this system, I need to know I won't run through an asteroid field and break my ship."

Hendrickson's face still showed her incomprehension, so Yager kept going.

"Who better to judge the spacing and feasibility of entering Aleph than the *Pike*'s primary navigator? You've got the experience, Shi, and I want your eyes on anything I'm going to ask you to fly us into."

Shi nodded. "Thank you, ma'am, for explaining."

Yager opened her mouth, then closed it and shook her head.

"Shi, sit down. I'm going to give you some advice. Good. Shi, you need to relax. No, I'm your captain now, and I'm trying to help, so wait until I'm done. Shi, it's not your fault." Yager raised her hand to stop the words before they started. "I know what happened. I can't say I know what it was like, because I wasn't there. But I know you did everything you could, and you blame yourself for not doing enough. Guess what?"

Hendrickson's face was a mask of confusion.

"What you did was enough because you lived. And if you hadn't been here, aboard the *Pike*, if it was some other nav? We'd all be as dead as your old crew. No, Shi, you couldn't save them. But you saved all of us, and if that's not good enough for you, then I don't know what is. Dismissed."

"LIEUTENANT, WELCOME TO the *Wodehouse*." Sergeant Everett Orellana welcomed Shi aboard the shuttle. He grinned at her. "We've installed a third seat in the cockpit so you can have a good view. Oh, and we added all the usual bells and whistles, so you have instruments and monitors."

"Thanks. Um, haven't I seen you in the mess?"

"We've had lunch a couple times," Orellana said.

"Then you'd better call me Shi."

"Rat."

"Rat?" she said. "How did you get that handle?"

"Well, when I was in training, my cohort found out my first name, and Rat was a better choice." He stopped. When it became clear he wouldn't say more, Shi shook her head and found her seat.

Pleasantries complete, they waited for Sergeant Zjhadse, the engineer, to finish her walkaround. The cockpit of the Wolf Mark II shuttle was cramped compared to the bridge of the *Pike*, but Shi felt surprisingly at ease. Zjhadse completed the preflight, and Orellana requested clearance.

"Ace, are we clear?"

The Pod AI responded, "You are, Rat. At eighteen light minutes, there's a meteoroid swarm on your planned course, bearing one twenty-two mark negative thirty-eight. Don't run into them, or you'll scratch the bird, and I won't be happy."

"No problem, Ace. Zapper, keep an eye out." The engineer nodded. Shi fastened the harnesses and brought her instruments online.

"Shi?"

Hendrickson looked up from the display.

"SOP. Suit integrity check."

Shi suppressed a shudder. Skinsuits were part of the uniform, worn at all times shipboard. They were comfortable and unobtrusive, easily forgotten, and not at all traumatic.

The helmet was another thing.

Shi hadn't worn a helmet more than a half-dozen times since the *Young*.

"Lieutenant?" Rat looked over his shoulder. "Not optional."

Hendrickson lifted the polycarbonate-coated optical sapphire sphere with a wince and set it on her shoulders. The smart fabric of her skinsuit noted its presence and secured the helmet to the suit.

"Pressure check," Shi said, and the suit circulated additional air. "Good."

"Sorry, Shi." Hendrickson heard Rat's voice over the comms. "Regulations."

"No problem, Rat. I keep it on?"

"You do," he said.

She could cope. She could. Just because it reminded her of rushing air and dead friends and . . .

Stop it!

Shi closed her eyes. Maybe one of Beckman's self-relaxation techniques would work for once.

"Crew secure. Launching," she heard Rat announce. With her eyes closed, Hendrickson was aware of the increased vibration in the shuttle's deck as Zapper brought the engines to power. It, too, brought her back to the *Young*. The *Pike*'s mass squelched any sense of movement aboard, but the *Young* had been only a little larger than a Wolf.

Her hands moved of their own accord. They traced patterns she hadn't used in five years, recalling the way she'd balanced the frigate at the edge of its abilities. For a moment, she could smell the acrid whiff of ozone that always permeated the bridge from a faulty connection the engineers could never track down, no matter how often Captain Gonzalez had them search. The rattle from her chair where a bolt refused to tighten fully. The bustle of the crew behind her, going about their business. A simpler time, before war and blood and death and pain.

Rat brought her back to the present with a lurch.

"Shi, we're starting our run. You ready?"

"Ready."

"RAT, WE'RE COMING UP on the meteors," Zapper said from her console. "Just where Ace said they'd be."

Rat grumbled, "Why are we going through here?"

"Shi?"

Hendrickson didn't look up from her plotting. "Because the rest of the system's a worse mess and gravity's a bitch-and-a-half."

"Why stop, then?" Zapper thought it was a reasonable question.

Now Shi tore her attention away from the plot. "There are three stars, two in a tidally locked pair, which orbits the third. That's pretty unusual. There's enough junk to make a fourth star. That makes the system valuable for raw materials. But the clincher, the reason the Captain's so hyped up about it, is because there's a Jovian orbiting the primary star."

"So? We run into Jovians all the time."

"Not when I'm flying!" Rat exclaimed.

"You know what I mean, frak-head," Zapper replied. "Seriously, we see Jovians in almost every system."

"Not with potentially habitable moons," Shi said.

"Really? Like Thalia's moons?"

"Exactly. It's totally out of left field, and nobody would believe us if we hadn't found it, but you know what the Old Lady says: facts trump theories."

Zapper whistled. "Okay. Makes sense." She turned back to her instruments.

"One light minute," Rat said. "Shields?"

"Online, for all the good they'll do."

Rat grunted. The new Wolves had electromagnetic shielding, which was terrific for distorting laser beams and deflecting charged particles. It did nothing to stop rocks and ice and other bits of debris. For that, they'd need gravitic shielding, but they didn't have the power. Hell, the *Pike* barely generated enough energy, and she packed more annie plants than any construction smaller than a habitat!

Lacking the gravitic shields, they made do with a layer of CeeSea, passivated chromium Seaborgium in crystalline metallic form. It was tough and dense and gave them some measure of protection against the physical hazards of space.

Rat wasn't complaining. He was glad to have anything, especially when deliberately steering into a cluster. He flipped the shuttle end-for-end and stabilized.

"Decelerating," he said, firing up the drive. The soothing, familiar vibration returned. "We'll enter at 50 kps."

"Fifty?" Shi asked. "Isn't that fast?"

Rat turned. "Not when I'm at the—"

He was cut off by a baseball-sized rock punching through the shield, CeeSea, duralloy hull, roof-mounted controls, most of his body, his seat, the deck, the main power conduit to the cockpit, and out the keel of the shuttle.

Every light went dead, leaving only the brilliant shine of Aleph A and the myriad stars, and Shi's mind went away.

THE LIGHTS FLICKERED AND DIED, then the gravity failed as well.

"We're getting hammered; Shi, get us out of here!" ordered Ballentine, firing her last missile. "Full power to the engines!"

"I'm trying," Shi answered, returning to her controls and blinking away the blurriness from her eyes. "Engines aren't answering commands."

"Weatherby, get a signal out to the *Defender*. We need assistance! Gods damn it!" Ballentine's order ended in a curse. Shi checked her own sensor readings and paled. The *Anders* was still there, but a larger signal was approaching: a Copernicus-class cruiser. No 400 kW lasers on this monster. They mounted four six-megawatt lasers on their spines and twenty-one–megawatt lasers in each broadside battery, as well as up to forty nuclear-tipped Huygens missiles.

"Blessed Mother save us," whispered Shi, still attempting to get a response from the engines.

SHI SNAPPED BACK, the memory fading, Zapper's rasps in her comms. She closed her eyes for a moment.

Not again! This can't be happening again!

The brilliant sparking of ruptured controls shone through her eyelids, and she forced herself to see. Flashing red alarm lights were the primary illumination, enough to see the cockpit.

Rat was well and truly dead.

Zapper looked little better, but the rise and fall of her chest showed.

"Okay, Shi. Don't panic."

She had to admit it sounded hollow in her own ears, but some part of her brain listened and reacted. Her heartbeat slowed, and her hands stopped trembling.

Well, if it's stupid and it works . . . Shi kept talking.

"I can't think! Shut down the damn alarm. Where? Got to be easy to find. There!" One large button on the forward console flashed in time with the lights, and she slapped it. The flashing died.

"Better. Next. What's running?"

The simple answer was not much.

"Suit. I can breathe. I'm not frozen. Comms? Local, at least. I can hear Zapper." Hendrickson undid her harness. "Gravity's still up," she said, checking the engineer.

"I think she's just knocked out. Zapper! Can you hear me?"

There was no response, so Shi reached for Zapper's arm and gave it a shake. Still nothing.

"Right, what else? Long-range comms? *Wodehouse* to *Pike*, come in, over."

The Q-Net the Terran Federation ran on provided instantaneous communications over extended distances. Everyone in the Fleet had an implant that could transmit a couple of light minutes. The Wolves mounted a larger transmitter, extending the range to light hours. Under normal circumstances, the implant would pick up her voice and then redirect to the appropriate broadcast system. Here, it would be the *Wodehouse*'s installation.

Which didn't seem to be doing anything.

"Frak me."

No comms, which meant no rescue any time soon.

Shi considered her situation. She needed control of the Wolf, and that meant one of the two stations in front of her. Rat's seat was trashed, and she'd have to move his body.

No thanks.

Which left Zapper's side. If she was going to do anything useful, she needed Zapper out of the way. It was a struggle, but Hendrickson undid the harness and lugged the unconscious engineer into the third seat.

"Damn," Shi said, panting. "Zapper, either you're heavier than you look, or I need to get back into the gym."

Shi checked Zapper's console next. Fortunately, the Wolves were designed to be operated after relatively brief training. No training made it a bit more challenging, but she piloted a four-kilometer-long ship. How tough could a thirty-five-meter-long shuttle be?

"Simple enough that even a nav can figure it out." Shi settled in. "Engines, in shutdown. Good, good, you don't need to keep accelerating. No, hold on, you want the engines on. Otherwise, you're going to keep heading in-system!"

She looked for the right controls to turn them on. The problem she encountered was all the controls were virtual, electronic representations on Zapper's console, rather than buttons and switches. Worse, the Wolves didn't have AIs integrated. Since the Q-Net transmitter was down, her implant didn't have the range to contact Hermes. That meant she had no helpful assistance at her mind's call.

"Think. Think! There are always redundancies, always secondary access, right? Right! Basic design, don't put all your eggs in one basket." She pondered, briefly, why you might want to put any eggs in a basket. "There has to be something, probably simple and obvious, like that big red switch!"

On the side of the console was a single button. Hendrickson mashed it.

The console rotated about its horizontal axis, and a panel of archaic analog dials, gauges, and sliders appeared. Hendrickson was exultant.

"Yes!"

Better yet, their functions were labeled.

"Power, power, power, there." She pushed the slider up to the 80 percent mark, the usual setting for full military power, and felt a reassuring rumble through her seat.

"Now, do I have any sensors?"

Her examination of the primary scan monitor revealed it had died an electronic death.

"I could probably rig it if I had time, but no, I have to get Zapper back to *Pike*," she said, moving on. "Flying blind. Fun. At least I'm pointed in the right direction."

A thought struck her, and she cast her eyes over the console. "How the hell do I steer?"

Shi glanced at the body of Rat. His controls looked intact, and unlike Zapper's, his were still stuck solidly in the twenty-first century: joystick on the right, throttle on the left, wait. Throttle?

She looked at the label on the slider she'd just used.

"Engine output? How is that different from a throttle?" Shi didn't have the slightest idea, so experimentation was in order. But to experiment, she needed a chair, and maybe one without a bloody great hole and a body. She unbuckled and shuffled across to Rat's station.

Eww.

"Sorry, Rat," she said. Shi pushed past his body and looked under the remains of the seat. "If they installed one for me, it has to have standard latches, quick-releases, if I can find them . . . Ah-ha!"

She tugged at a latch. After a moment's resistance, it popped open, and the corner of the chair shifted. Hendrickson looked to the back, found a similar latch, and tugged again. This one was more challenging, but it too released. She shuffled around the back of the seat and undid the latch on the left side.

"One to go. Oh, shit."

The impact had warped the remaining latch, and Shi knew she couldn't get it undone by hand.

"I need a tool," she muttered. "Where would I put tools?"

Shi turned and looked at the bulkhead.

"Gods, I love the engineering mind," she said, surprising herself with a laugh. An outline of red dashes showed a large hatch. Clinching the deal, "Emergency Kit" was stenciled in the center. She pulled the handle, and it popped open.

"Wrench? Hammer? Why do they have a crowbar? Locking grips!"

Shi pulled out the tool. She examined the twisted latch and clamped it into place.

She felt a long, groaning vibration through her feet which froze her in place. The red lights started their manic dance again, and she slapped the same button.

"I wonder what happened?" The cockpit was still intact, for values of intact. They must have taken another hit, maybe in the passenger compartment, perhaps on one of the stubby wings.

"At least we have no more atmosphere to vent," she mused, wondering where this sense of humor came from. Not that she was questioning it. Right now, it felt good to smile, no matter how grim the subject matter.

Now she felt an irregularity to the engine's output.

"Not good, not good, *so* not good." Shi abandoned the chair for now and returned to Zapper's station. "Damnation."

Wolves ran on a fusion reactor and relied on a stable magnetic bottle to keep the super-heated hydrogen and helium in place. It wasn't as dangerously unstable as an annie plant. The reaction would stop long before the bottle failed, instead of an uncontrolled matter/antimatter mix. But if the fusion plant died, so did the engines.

"Maybe not so bad," she said. "Maybe we've killed our accel. Ah, crap."

Nope. She was still heading in-system. Slower, now, but still 6 kps.

"Maybe . . ."

Shi reached for the engine output control and started pulling it down, feeling for any changes in the irregular thrum through her feet. It eased as she reduced the demand on the reactor.

Seventy.

Sixty.

Fifty.

Forty.

Thirty.

The vibration was almost imperceptible now, and she checked the readings.

Twenty-eight.

"One percent fluctuation." She dug into the long-ago engineering familiarization courses she'd endured, dredged up a number she liked, and locked the control in place.

"That's going to suck," she said, then shrugged. She was still reducing her speed by seven hundred meters per second, which was something. Hendrickson returned to the recalcitrant latch. One solid wrench and it popped loose. Rat's body, and the chair, tumbled backward, and she winced.

The chair and grisly cargo were disconcertingly easy to drag out of the cockpit, where Shi saw the latest damage.

"Frak me running," she whispered. A massive rock was wedged against the bent and mangled bulkhead, which separated the passenger area from the engine. A quick look upward, and Shi was looking into space, the roof accordioned back from the front of the compartment. The meteor must have had only the slightest difference in velocity, plowing through on mass rather than speed.

She shivered and involuntarily closed her eyes.

SHI'S CONSOLE BLEW APART in front of her. Her skinsuit blunted the buffeting of the plastic and metal shards even as it transmitted the force to her body. She grunted in pain before blacking out.

She groaned, recovering consciousness, and then opened her eyes.

Why am I so heavy? she wondered, then remembered. *We should have stopped. Why haven't we stopped?*

She looked around. The lights were gone again, the only illumination from sparks and flickers from the ruined controls around the bridge. Through the hole in the bulkhead, she could see the stars moving.

"NO!" HENDRICKSON FORCED HER EYES open again and screamed in protest. "Gods damn me, nobody else dies!"

She left Rat and returned to the cockpit. Zapper's chair shifted quickly, and she installed herself in the makeshift pilot's seat.

"So simple a nav can do it," she said again. "Course heading, course heading, ah, here!" The readout showed her the current trajectory relative to Aleph A. Now, where was the *Pike*? Shi closed her eyes again, willing the coordinates to appear from her last duty shift.

Gotcha!

Triumphantly, she opened her eyes and compared her memory to the course. Not exact; there had been some drift, but pretty close.

"Considering I'm flying a bird with two frakking great holes in it, not bad," she mused. She placed a hand on the joystick and gave it a tentative shake. She saw the stars wobble through the cockpit window.

"Hey, something's working!" Encouraged, she pushed the throttle forward, increasing the reactor's output to the engines. The inertial compensator muted the effect, holding internal gravity at 0.75 g, and Hendrickson released a long-held breath. If the compensators went bad, she'd be so much paste on the bulkhead.

"Nope, you are not thinking that way. Okay, seventeen light minutes, that's three hundred million kilometers. Still, I don't have to cover all that, only two-seventy, then I can yell for help on my implant." Shi did a bit more mental math. At 700 mps acceleration, she was looking at . . .

"Shit. Eleven hours."

She considered this, then shrugged.

"Not like I have anything better to do. Course steady, reactor output steady, and we're on track." Shi examined the panel. "I don't suppose there's any way I can put this thing on autopilot? I might be asking too much, but don't I deserve something to go my way?"

A control promised exactly that, but didn't respond to Hendrickson's manipulation.

"Hands-on flying, I guess," she said and settled in. "Wish I'd loaded some of Admiral Cassidy's vids to my implant."

ZAPPER'S SCREAM PULLED SHI out of her doze. She turned to see what happened. The straps still held Zapper in place, but she waved her arms, eyes closed, and yelled, "No! No!"

Hendrickson made a quick check of their course before unbuckling.

"Zapper! Zjadhse!" She put her hands on the stricken engineer's shoulders, hoping the pressure, the touch of another person, would bring her out of it.

"Zjadhse!" Shi repeated. "Come on, come on, I'm here. Come back," she said, putting as much comfort into her voice as she could manage.

Zapper's eyes fluttered open and focused on Shi's face.

"Lieu-lieutenant?"

"That's right, Lieutenant Hendrickson. Shi. You remember?"

Zapper nodded. "What . . . ?" She raised her hands to her head, found the helmet in the way, and started to remove it.

"No!" Shi snapped, stopping Zapper's hands. "Don't take off your helmet!"

She softened her tone. "We're in vacuum. What do you remember?"

"Vacuum? Uh, I, I don't know. We were closing on the swarm, and then . . ." Zapper paused, then shook her head. "That's all I have."

Shi nodded. "How do you feel?"

"My head hurts. It feels like my brain's trying to get out," Zapper said with a weak smile.

"Your nanobots aren't handling it?"

Zapper's eyes closed as she accessed the interface. Her implant controlled her 'bots, down at the same level as her autonomic nervous system. Like breathing, she could change it if she concentrated, but it required an effort of will.

"Crap," Zapper said a moment later. "They're already on it."

"There's not much more I can do." Shi returned to the seat and checked on their course. Still on track. She concentrated on her work, hoping Zapper wouldn't ask the questions she knew were coming.

"Um. Lieutenant? Shi?"

"Hmm?"

"Why are you piloting? Why am I in your chair? Where's Rat?"

And there they were.

Shi would tell her the truth, if not all the details. They could wait.

"We had an accident, and Rat didn't make it. We're on the way home. A few more hours."

"Rat didn't make it?"

"No. It was quick." Shi was sure of that.

Zapper fell silent. After a few minutes, Shi broke the quiet.

"Zapper?"

"I'm here," came the dull response. Shi wasn't surprised; it was exactly as she'd reacted for the years after the *Young*.

"Zjadhse, I know you're not ready to hear this, but you need to. There wasn't anything you could do. Nothing. Shit happens, especially when you get into the black, and there's no margin for error." Shi's eyes were watering, and the controls were blurring, but she needed to continue. "Believe me, Zjadhse. I know."

"How?" choked Zapper.

Taking a deep breath, Shi told her, from beginning to end, the first person she'd told the entire truth to. Ever.

It took her over an hour of fits and starts, of self-interruption, of nearly forgotten details. She relived the sights and sounds, the pain and the horror, her heartbreak and agony, and the terrible decision not to allow herself to drift into space. When she finished, both women were crying, which was a pain in the ass when you were in vacuum and couldn't blot your eyes.

"Damn," Zapper said.

"About right," Hendrickson agreed. "It's hell. And you're going to go through your own, but I promise you, Zjadhse, you'll come out."

They fell silent again, the battered Wolf making its best time for where Shi hoped the *Pike* was.

"... *WODEHOUSE*, CAN YOU hear me?"

"This is Lieutenant Hendrickson aboard the *Wodehouse*," Shi said excitedly. "I hear you! Zapper! It's the *Pike*!"

"Shi? Is that you?" Shi had never interacted much with Ensign Baldwin, but she'd never been so happy to hear anyone her entire life.

"How many Hendrickson's do you know, Mike?" She shook her head. Ensigns!

"Patching you to the Old Lady." There was a pause, and then Captain Yager's voice was on the comm.

"Lieutenant? You're overdue."

Shi ignored the implied criticism and request for information. "Captain, we need an escort in and medical as soon as we land. I have casualties and no time to give you a report."

Yager responded the way Shi hoped she would.

"How can we help, Shi?"

"We're still an hour out. Reactor damage."

"Understood. We'll vector for intercept, get you home sooner."

"Thank you, Captain."

"Medical will be waiting. Captain Marsh will have Direwolves watch your back."

"Thank you, Captain. I'll fill you in when I'm aboard and showered. Hendrickson out."

"LIEUTENANT HENDRICKSON? Your appointment isn't until next Tuesday."

Shi smiled at the Commander. "I won't be here. I wanted to stop by and tell you in person rather than just shoot you a message. You were right, by the way."

Genesis quirked an eyebrow and said, "I was?"

"You were. I needed to talk about it."

"I'm assuming you did?"

Shi nodded.

"And it helped?"

"You know, I think it did."

Genesis stood. "My door is always open, Lieutenant."

"Nothing personal, but I won't be using it." With a pleased grin, Shi walked out.

SHI JERKED UPRIGHT, eyes wide and unseeing. Where was the wolf? It wasn't there. It wasn't anywhere she could see, hear, or feel.

She leaned back onto her pillow, closed her eyes, and drifted back to sleep, her ghosts at peace.

The wolf skulked away to seek easier prey.

Child's Play

DAWN VOGEL

Dawn Vogel has written for children, teens, and adults, spanning genres, places, and time periods. More than a hundred of her stories and poems have been published by small and large presses. Her specialties include young protagonists, siblings who bicker but love each other in the end, and things in the water that want you dead. She is a member of the Science Fiction & Fantasy Writers Association and Codex Writers. She lives in Seattle with her awesome husband (and fellow author), Jeremy Zimmerman, and their cats. Visit her at historythatneverwas.com or on BlueSky @historyneverwas.

IF THE KIDS HADN'T TAKEN MY HELMET, I wouldn't have tracked them down. I was injured and needed to rest. But if I didn't get it back, the kids would have some nasty people looking for them, thinking they'd have the chance to put me down for good.

I slapped on my last painkiller patch. It would be enough to take the edge off, hopefully for long enough to find my stolen gear.

My pursuers had tech to track me, via the helmet the kids had taken. I'd hijacked my way into that tech, so I'd also tracked my helmet to Ducktown, a junkyard where amphibious landing crafts, "ducks," had their final resting place amidst a graveyard of everything else that no longer had a purpose.

Based on the tracker readings I got, I had about half an hour before the people after me could get here. They'd likely come in guns blazing. I left my ship in a nearby canyon, hidden enough they'd overlook it in their haste. But I couldn't waste any time.

Ducktown was almost impenetrable from the ground, with towers of junk ringing it like a fortress wall. There were gaps, if you knew where to look for them. And if you weren't afraid of the whole damn place coming down on your head if you bumped into the wrong pile.

I followed the sounds of play to a clearing beyond the gap. The kids were playing catch with the helmet. I hadn't gotten a good look at them when they'd taken it. They were smaller—younger—than I'd expected. Nimble little things.

The painkiller patch was doing its job, but I was in no condition to take my helmet back by force. And I don't kill kids.

But even kids would trade a toy for something they wanted more. I emerged into the clearing with my hands up.

"Hey, you willing to trade?" I asked, eyeing the helmet.

The kid holding the helmet looked like he'd rolled in dirt for every bit of color on his body. Even his teeth looked dusty brown. "What for, lady?"

I twisted to show them my satchel. "I got about a week's worth of ration bars in here."

"Gross," he spat back. "Got anything better than that?"

I shook my head. "There are people on their way here right now who want that thing, and if you let me take it now, they won't bother you. They'll come after me instead."

"They can't get into Ducktown," the younger girl—all curly red hair and a mess of freckles standing out on her much cleaner and paler skin—shouted, defiant.

"They're not gonna care if the junk comes down around them. And they're not going to be nice about taking it, either."

"You got guns?" the boy asked, crossing one arm over his chest, holding my helmet at his side.

I grimaced, not only because the painkiller patch wasn't keeping pace with the pain. "I'm not giving you a gun, kid."

"Why not?"

"Because kids and guns don't mix."

"You're no fun."

I eyed them both. "What are your names?"

"I'm Petey. She's Lyss. What's your name?"

"Starwitch."

Petey narrowed his eyes. "That's not a real name."

"Oh? It's what people call me, so I think that counts."

"I want people to call me Princess," Lyss said, "but Princess Gunslinger would be really cool."

I smiled. "Maybe someday, kiddo."

From above came the whine of ships incoming. My gaze darted up. A wave of vertigo followed, and I stumbled backward.

"Are you okay, Starwitch?" Petey asked.

I didn't get a chance to answer his question, as my stumble turned into a case of the ground rushing up to meet my face.

I COULDN'T TELL HOW LONG I'd been out, but when I woke up, my helmet was in front of me, reflecting my drawn, pale face. I was in the shade of two towering junk piles, but looking up at them spun up the vertigo again, so I pressed my eyes closed.

Something brushed up against my arm, and I flailed for it.

"Shh," a voice whispered.

"Who's there?"

"Lyss. Stay quiet. The bad people landed."

"Where's Petey?"

"Hiding across the way. He'll distract them if they come this way."

I was glad to hear both the kids had at least listened to me about the danger these people would put them in.

Something solid skittered across the ground in the distance.

"Check that way," a gruff voice barked. "Don't stop tracking the chip."

The chip, which was inside the helmet, which was beside my head.

"Lyss, I need you to hide farther away from me."

"Nuh-uh."

"They're going to find me."

"Nuh-uh."

"Hey, butt monkeys!" That was Petey. The way his voice echoed, he was back in the clearing, not hiding amongst the junk. Dammit.

Blasters powered up.

Lyss brushed against my holster, which felt lighter now.

I fumbled for her arm but touched only air. "Lyss, no. Come back with that."

"Don't shoot him," she yelled, her voice not wavering an ounce.

Both these kids were about to get themselves killed.

"Junkyard rats," came another adult voice. "If it's here, it's probably buried somewhere. I don't think she'd have stuck around."

"You're trespassing," Petey said. "Get outta Ducktown."

A heavy footfall echoed through the clearing.

Petey yelped.

"Give me the helmet," the first gruff voice intoned.

Struggling against the vertigo, I pulled myself to a seated position, then started to get my legs under me. Lyss might have had my six-shooter, but I had other weapons.

I grabbed for a throwing knife but came up empty. Forcing my eyes open, I looked down into the empty sheath in my boot. Damn, this kid had cleaned me out!

A pistol shot rang out. It was high, a few meters off the ground.

Lyss stood at the end of the narrow junk aisle, both hands holding the pistol well over her head, aimed at the sky, the tip smoking. In silhouette, she looked like a much younger me, playing with my dad's guns.

Only she had better aim than me at that age.

"Lyss," I hissed at her, gesturing for her to come back, out of sight of my pursuers.

"They're going," she mouthed.

Another wave of vertigo washed over me, and I found myself headed back to the ground.

GUNSHOTS WOKE ME the second time.

They were followed by a tinkle of glass and punctuated with laughter and childish shouts.

I crawled toward the clearing, not trusting my legs.

There were no more gruff voices, no more menacing air. It sounded like children playing.

With my gun.

And my ammo.

"Hey," I called when I reached the clearing. "I told you, no guns."

"We scared off the bad people," Lyss said, hand on one hip, my pistol aimed toward the sky again.

"And I appreciate that."

Petey eyed me. "You've got the helmet, and we've got your pistol. That's a fair trade, right?"

"No, not really," I replied. "Tell you what. You got anyone here with a medkit?"

Petey nodded.

"You get me a painkiller patch, and once I'm feeling a little better, I'll take the tracking chip out of the helmet. Then you can keep it, but I get my pistol back." I glanced at Lyss. "And my knives?"

"I only took them so you wouldn't stab yourself on accident," she said, gesturing to the pile at the clearing's edge.

"Well. Thanks for rescuing me."

Petey looked at the pistol in Lyss's hand, then looked at my helmet. "What do you think, Lyss?"

"I still want a gun."

"Maybe when you're older, kid," I said.

She looked at me, eyes shining. "How old?"

I wasn't good at guessing kids' ages, but I knew what age she wasn't near. "Fifteen."

Her shoulders slumped. "That's forever away!"

I suspected these kids wouldn't take no for an answer. And someday, they'd find someone to give them a gun. Maybe I could forestall them from getting something that would get them killed.

I knew a guy who specialized in non-lethal weaponry, the kind that shot rubber pellets and the like. Yeah, you could still hurt someone with them at close range, but maybe these kids would be alright with something like that. There were good reasons to encourage Lyss to keep her skills sharp, too. She wouldn't be a kid forever.

"Okay, I'll sweeten the pot." Holding up fingers as I ticked off the points, I said, "Pain patch and my gun for me. Helmet for you now, and I'll come back with some pellet guns—only for shooting junk, not each other—in a week or two."

"Promise?" Lyss asked, her eyes wide.

"Cross my heart and hope to die," I replied.

Both kids grinned. "Deal."

Cold Cowardice

WESLEY ZUROVEC

> Wesley Zurovec lives in Austin, Texas, where he devotes time to writing short fiction, playing board games, and coaching his kids' sports teams. His stories have appeared in Roi Fainéant Press; *ScribesMICRO*; *Suddenly, and Without Warning*; and other publications. Find him on X @WRZurovec.

THEY LOOKED LIKE ANTS when we first saw them coming. Marching, marching, marching, gradually getting taller and closer. Black dots against the white snow. At least twenty of them for every one of us, that's what the drones reported. Captain said we'd never stand a chance against a whole damn army. As if we didn't already know.

The snow, laid out like a rug in front of us, started disappearing under all those marching feet. That pure, untrodden white was all the time we had left.

Why had the enemy come to this desolate, frozen planet? The war was all but over; they must have known that by now. And we were just an ordinary communications outpost of relatively few men and no strategic importance. What would they gain by killing a couple dozen more of us?

I LET MY MIND wander.

Closed my eyes and thought about Patty and the kids and our life and things left undone. The barn roof still leaked and needed replacing. The hinges on the back gate were all busted up and cockeyed from when the bull got into it. Worse, I'd only half-finished the boys' treehouse when the governor ordered me to return to action. That was two years ago.

Then, somehow, for just a moment, I felt the warmth of our fireplace and the morning coffee and the sun rising up high over the pecan trees so bright and crisp and comfortable.

I thought of Patty.

THE WIND WAS COLDER now than before. Men were anxious. We still had time to load up into the transport pods and blast ourselves into orbit away from this mess. So Captain took out his thermal blade. He made a line thirty feet long in the packed snow.

"Anyone wants to leave, go ahead and step across."

No one moved.

Seemed like time itself froze up after Captain spoke. Everyone was watching everybody else to see who'd step forward first. My feet wouldn't budge, like they were frozen, too.

I didn't want to stay there and die. I was just too afraid to admit to the others that I wanted to keep on living.

Before I could muster my courage, time got going again. Captain said something else about honor or valor. The men gave a muffled cheer, went back to their posts, and that was it.

Didn't any of us care about what we'd be leaving behind? Back home, I mean. Here, all we'd be leaving behind were bodies.

THERE WASN'T MUCH SNOW left between us and the enemy by sundown. That's when the chirping began. Louder and louder as the sky grew darker and darker. Even though we'd never heard anything like it before, we knew it was a death song. The sentries announced that the threat was close enough to engage. A few men vomited. It was the first time any of us had seen the creatures in the flesh, and we were not prepared to behold the horrors drawing nearer with each falling snowflake.

We warmed up our hands at the fire then hitched the fuel tanks to the backs of our insulated pressure suits. Everyone lined up and filed through the outer gate. Except for me. Captain came back and grabbed ahold of my arm and pulled me out into the darkness. "Torch as many as you can!" Then he ran on ahead, and I was alone.

OUR FLAMETHROWERS LIT UP the black sky, lit up everything orange, and I wish you could've seen those bastards dance. Twisting, screaming, jumping around like a bunch of burning crickets, all charred black and curling up on the snow. Antennas quivering in the heat. Venomous stingers and fangs melting like candles. Hardened exoskeletons rendered useless against our fires. One after another, after another, after another they fell.

It was the first time I'd felt good since leaving home. Like I was making a real difference, at last.

AND THEN THE FLAMETHROWERS started cutting off one by one as our fuel ran out. The darkness came back. Cold, nauseating, paralyzing darkness, inside and out. My feet wouldn't move, frozen like before, and then my arms wouldn't move either. I closed my eyes and tried to think of anything else as the evil swarmed all around me. But I couldn't think or even hardly breathe, so I knelt down in the snow and sat still and prayed. The taste of death on my tongue, I could see nothing in the darkness. Nothing except all those glowing eyes closing in.

There wasn't any point in pulling out my thermal blade.

I let them kill me just as they did everyone else, fighters and cowards alike.

It was inevitable.

IN SPITE OF ALL THAT, the enemy leaders surrendered only two weeks later, around the same time that word of what had happened to us reached Patty. The terms were all but finalized even before we'd met our fate. There'd been a paperwork delay, apparently.

MY KIDS REMEMBER ME as a war hero. A valiant defender of mankind. That's how their kids will know me, too. I'm not sure how Patty sees things, exactly. Seems she's too busy raising the kids and keeping things running around the house to dwell on it much anymore.

None of them knows about the line drawn in the snow, about the choice I was given and how I froze up, how easily I could've come home, except for being too frightened. Would them knowing make any difference? They didn't feel the judgment in the eyes of the other soldiers that day. They didn't see all the other eyes, thousands of them, cruel and glowing in the darkness. They didn't watch me kneel down in defeat at the end.

My kids don't realize that I threw my life away for nothing, though I think Patty might suspect it from time to time when the sun sets low behind the pecan trees and the crickets wake up and start their night songs.

The Final Float

Kevin Brown

Kevin Brown has published two short story
collections, *Death Roll* and *Ink On Wood*, and has had
fiction, nonfiction, and poetry published in over 200
literary journals, magazines, and anthologies. He
has won numerous writing competitions and been
nominated for multiple prizes and awards, including
three Pushcart Prizes.

"THAT IT?" KYSON SAID. He pointed at a wall of thickets and timbered old-growth dense as the rest of the woods surrounding them. An overgrown road disappeared inside it.

"Is what it?" Brodie said, raising his shades and squinting through the back glass.

Kyson held the napkin up, slid his eyes from the scratched directions to the road and back. He angled it right, spun it left, then balled it up and dropped it on the floorboard.

Brodie shrugged and slipped his shades back down. Threw the pick-up in reverse, pulled onto the road, and started in.

The pitch was sharp, the truck bouncing over oak roots knotted in the road. Branches scraped the sides of the vehicle, the windows, the cab.

Slivers of sun-silvered river flared through holes in the canopied bush. Pieces of a building appeared and disappeared.

"Money," Brodie said.

"Ever any doubt?" Kyson said, gripping the "oh shit" handle. But he'd started to doubt. Began to think the place didn't exist. It wasn't on a map, not even close to another road on the map. And though he and Brodie had floated different rivers the last couple years, they'd never heard of this one. It was the weird old guy at Mason's Pub that told them about the place. The Rotten Oar. Overheard Kyson and Brodie talking about a two-day float and slid down to the stool next to them.

"You never had a float like it," he said, a wiry beard veined by a braid of scar along his jawline. "Life changing."

He scrawled drunken directions on a beer-damp napkin and three days later they were here.

At the bottom of the road it smoothed and opened to an old house and a large, weather-flaked barn. Behind the barn, a cluster of decrepit sheds.

"Rotten Oar Floats" was painted in red childlike letters above the open barn door. They pulled in, got out, and looked around.

The house was bowed in the middle. A dead maple had grown through the front porch, the top lying over the rusted tin roof. The breeze waved a shutter back and forth like a sleepy blinking eye.

"Don't look like much to me," Kyson said. He adjusted his tilley hat and said, "Anybody even here?"

Looking around, Brodie spat, leaned in the truck, and laid on the horn.

A soft echo.

He hit it again.

Cicadas screamed. There was a junkyard behind the sheds. Hollowed out vehicles, rusted through and gutted with weeds.

"Help you?" a scratchy voice said, from the dark of the barn. A large man appeared, staring as if he'd never seen customers before. He was bald except for a tuft of white hair above one ear. He wore an unbuttoned shirt, and a purple, rope thick scar ran from his naval over his breastbone. Up his throat and chin, splitting his bottom lip in a meaty wet V.

Kyson looked away. Said: "You rent canoes?" The man looked over his shoulder at the sign, then back at Kyson without speaking.

"We're gonna need one," Brodie said, slow. "And a shuttle upriver. 'Bout two days' worth."

The man ran his eyes over them and looked out at the river. "Why don't you boys go somewheres else to do your floating?"

"Good sales pitch," Kyson said, to himself.

Brodie's jaw tightened. "We were told this is the float to take," he said. "Took us three days to find it, so . . ."

The man breathed heavy, spittle whistling from his lip, and scratched at the scar. Shook his head and disappeared inside the barn. There was a loud thump, two slaps of wood-on-wood, and he reappeared, dragging a long oak canoe. It was warped and sun bleached, dark stains pock-marking the wood. One gunwhale was busted, and the hull was splintered and riddled with holes patched with sap. Inside were two bowed oars.

"Lives up to its name," Kyson said. "This thing even float?"

"It's a boat, ain't it?" the man said.

"Not really."

"It'll work," Brodie said. "What do we owe you?"

"Hundred a head," the man said.

"A hundred?" Kyson said.

Brodie held his hand up.

Kyson walked over and looked out at the river. The sun threw a million diamonds on the surface, and thirty yards up it ribboned off and out of sight, its skin wrinkled in the breeze.

Brodie paid and the man disappeared inside the barn.

"Two hundred bucks?" Kyson said.

"We're here," Brodie said, unloading the cooler. "Let's just be here."

Kyson grabbed the fishing rods. "Better be a hell of a float."

Brodie winked. "Always is."

The man pulled out in a truck with tattered screens bellied out for windows. He squeaked to a stop and stared ahead. Motor idling, brown exhaust streaming from the tailpipe.

"Hundred each," Kyson said, "and we load the damn canoe."

"I'm just ready to be on the water."

They loaded.

The cab floor was rusted out, the seat cushion-less, its springs shot.

"Guess we're in back," Kyson said.

They hopped in. The gears ground and they jerked toward the road they'd come down on, nosed up and disappeared into the land-scape.

The truck rocked to a halt.

They dusted leaves from their laps. Exposed skin was red-welted from two hours of biting twigs, clawing briers.

It was five feet from the embankment to the water, and Brodie jumped in, knee deep, and extended an arm.

Kyson eased the boat over the lip, grunting as the weight took hold, and it dropped, smacking wings of water out the sides. He turned, and the man was standing nose to nose with Kyson, breath whistling through the lip. "Ten miles in, you'll come to a V," he said. "You're gonna wanna keep to the right." He sucked in a string of spit and swallowed, his Adam's apple rolling up, then down beneath the scar. "That's the float you're here for."

"You bet," Kyson said. He stepped back and climbed down into the warm water.

The man stood over him, staring down.

Grabbing a tree trunk, they flung mud-slimed feet over the side and launched. It wobbled and they dipped their oars, bracing it. Eased out, absorbed by that first buoyant glide of a river's slither.

"Hear that?" the old man yelled. Kyson looked back. He stood facing the woods across the river. "Keep to the right!"

"Hell's that about?" Kyson said. As the thickets eclipsed the embankment, the man threw his head back, cupped his hands around his mouth, and screamed, "I told 'em!"

And he was gone.

The boil took them. Began to spin the stern perpendicular to the river, but Brodie dug left as Kyson pried the stern right, straightening it. A perfect cadence. The product of many miles and many currents.

The chop turned to foamy rapids that lifted the nose, then dipped it, a spray washing over them.

It rose and dipped. Smooth, rolling.

The landscape slid backwards. Opened up, then constricted.

The run pushed them around a bend and Kyson backwatered hard. Brodie threw his head back and howled.

"Hell yeah!" Kyson screamed, looking ahead at a grid of standing waves. The head troughed and the stern lifted, raising him off his seat, before the bow crested and sat him down. Then it calmed, the green water shoaling into an eddy.

Brodie palm-to-jaw popped his neck. "Not bad."

They coasted along, paddling in intervals. Boots submerged in a couple inches of water that had leaked through the resin. The surface went light green, then brown as the water shallowed over a riffle.

"Warm beer me," Brodie said. Kyson reached in the melted water of the cooler for a couple beers. He took a sip. Brodie bubbled his hard.

The water darkened again and they placed their oars across their laps. To the left, a fish rolled and disappeared. "Let's get some dinner," Brodie said, and grabbed his pole. Baited the hook with a fly and cast, letting it drag.

The sun was wide and unblocked in the sky. Soft-shell turtles stuck to the banks like wet cobblestones, and loggerheads sat motionless on the trunks of downed trees. A water moccasin S'ed past them upriver, its head raised. The soft current split around a boulder in the center of the river like white lace and the glassy surface of the water threw everything back on itself.

Brodie finished his beer, crushed the can, and peeled his wet shirt off.

Kyson stared at the "U.S.M.C." tattoo in Old English across his back. He'd just gotten it a couple days ago and it was still puffy and red.

"You nervous?" Kyson said.

"Not looking forward to all those needles." He reeled in, cast again. "Can't wait for boot camp, though."

Kyson knew this. Since junior high, Brodie had been preparing for the Marine Corps. The last couple years it'd become an obsession. He read *Soldier of Fortune*, quoted *Full Metal Jacket*, and worked out constantly, dieting until he was pads-on-pads of hard muscle layered in veins. He ran five miles before sunup every morning, rain or shine, sick or well. He'd tried to get Kyson to enlist on the buddy system. Even had a recruiter come see him. The Corps paid for college and you'd make good money and see the world. But Kyson did the math, and the good money he'd be making came out to about $350 a week. And the world he'd be seeing would be places the locals shoot at you. Plus, Kyson had been accepted at the University of Virginia, and that was world enough. So he passed. And though he'd miss his best friend since before He-Man was wimpy, he wasn't about to go die in a desert for minimum wage.

Brodie was about to take a drink when the rod bent, the line whining.

He snagged back and worked it, and within a few minutes, the pale trout was beside the boat, thrashing. He palmed it, dislodged the hook, and tossed it in the bottom. It flopped upright in the crude-whittled keel line and tried to swim in the sloshing water.

"We'll eat tonight," Brodie said, and slipped his tactical knife from its sheath. He smiled, and for a second, Kyson saw him as he used to—his buddy, wide-eyed and camo-ed with dirt. Who'd always be there tomorrow with some new idea or adventure to follow. Hard to believe this might be the last trip. Say a war doesn't get him, they'd both meet new friends, move on. It all felt like the end, like their river had reached the sea.

Kyson finished his beer, rigged his pole, and said, "Let me show you how a real angler does it."

They made camp on a rock bar with an oxbow lake arced behind it. It was the last flat bank before the landscape began to rise. The cliffs ahead were white, the tops limned with trees. The sun hovered just above, backlighting them.

Clouds the color of wet tissue stretched apart in the distance.

They each cleared a section of rocks for a bed and made small, makeshift lean-tos. They started a fire in a pit ringed with river stones, drank, and skipped shale. The water was dark except for a froth of small whitecaps that smoothed off and eddied on.

Kyson was drunk and seeing the world twinned. He cupped a handful of water over his face, the back of his neck. He was burnt, the skin on his nose and shoulders tight and sore. "Got warm."

"Gonna get chilly," Brodie said, and pointed at the clouds.

The sun flatlined over the rim of the cliffs.

After a while, they removed the fish from the stringer (Kyson had struck out, but Brodie had landed another). They gutted them, then ran sticks through the bellies and out the mouths. Their red and green tint glimmered over the flames. They sat on rocks, sipping hot beers and yawning.

A steady breeze kicked up, rattling the leaves. The smell of honeysuckle in its wake.

"Guess we might not get to do this again," Kyson said.

"I'll be back." Brodie took his fish from the flame, pinched a piece off. "It's only four years."

Kyson held his fish to his lips, blew, and took a bite, the fluffy white meat like cotton. "Remember the real American hero?"

Brodie smiled.

"You never admitted when I killed you?"

"You never did," Brodie said. "Cobra can hit a Joe, but he can't kill him." They laughed.

After a minute, Kyson stopped. "They drop you off over there," he said, "you can get killed."

"I can kill back, too."

They sat, fire popping and the river sliding by, black and fluid.

"'Bout the eighth week of camp, your dick'll be so hard you can't blink."

Brodie smiled, said: "I get out, I feel sorry for the first mess hall I chow at. She'll see what one motivated Marine and his gun can do."

"Kristi Spark?"

"Hell no! Titties look like two raw eggs on a door nail."

"Like putty in panty hose."

"Marbles in a condom."

They laughed and Kyson raised his can. "To counting down but not counting out," he said. "Semper fi, baby!"

Brodie raised his can. "Oorah!"

Heat lightning lit up the landscape. A distant rumble of thunder. The wind picked up, making a lip of waves crumble over the beach. A few drops of rain popped the surface of the river.

"Roughing it tonight," Brodie said.

"Any other way?"

Another flicker and the rain looked like ghost fingers thumping the water's surface.

It began to fall hard and they huddled under their lean-tos. The fire hissed and fluttered but didn't go out. After a half-hour, the storm slackened and moved on, its only evidence the occasional wink of light and low grind of thunder disappearing upriver. The moon slid out.

They lay soaked in the mud, Kyson staring out at the fire.

"Brodie?"

He groaned.

"Who you think that old bastard was yelling at?"

"Don't know," Brodie said, voice dragging. "Bet he don't, either."

"Weird," Kyson said.

"Forget him. He's miles off."

"More ways than one," Kyson said, and closed his eyes.

A DISTANT SCREAM SNAPPED him awake.

Moonlight filtered through the twigs of the lean-to, tiger-striping his face. It took a second to realize where he was.

There was a deep moan from the other side of the river.

Kyson rolled out, his insides novacained. Clothes wet and heavy.

"Brodie?" he said, but Brodie wasn't there. The embers in the fire pit glowed, and he stoked them and threw tinder on, and it lit up Brodie's silhouette, shin-deep in the water near the end of the bar. Motionless, staring up at the cliffs.

"The hell is that?" Kyson said, running toward him.

Another scream broke, with a grumbled answer from the left wall, a wailed response from the right, zigzagging farther downriver.

"Animals?" Kyson said, and held his breath.

"Don't think so."

They heard the screams another few minutes.

They didn't sleep the rest of the night.

LIGHT CAME, AND THE LAND BEGAN to form and take shape. One large instant picture shaken until it developed. A natural chiaroscuro, mist smoked over the river. Somewhere in the distance, the sound of runoff.

After the screams stopped, they'd sat in silence. Brodie watching the cliffs. Kyson keeping the fire alive. His clothes gripped him, chilling him to the marrow, and his body ached from too much beer under too much sun. He washed his face and drank from the river, shivering.

"Hell with it," he said, voice sandpapered whetstone. "Getting a hangover beer." The first drink was hard, but he put it away and began to feel better.

Brodie tipped the canoe, drained the water, and righted it. Following his lead, Kyson loaded the gear. He pissed on the coals, then swept stones over the pit with the side of his boot, and they slid the boat to the water's edge and pushed off.

The mist was a gauzy cataract around them. Brodie dug hard, cross-stroking in a scattershot rhythm, and Kyson struggled to control the yaw.

"You okay?" Kyson said.

No response.

"Brodie?"

"Just want some action's all."

The cliffs rose around them like a serpent's jaws. Large headwalls that cricked Kyson's neck when he looked up too long. The facing was pocked and pitted like acne scars.

"Could've been that old bastard," Kyson said. "Jerking us around."

"Maybe," Brodie said.

They wound on, Kyson drinking more and buzzing again. The sun burned the mist away. The water was deeper and a deeper shade of green.

After an hour or so, they came upon a spine of large boulders, dark and slick, that rose and disappeared in the water like a sea dragon's body.

"What you think?" Kyson said. "I don't trust that clit-lipped bastard."

"Trust or not, he don't scare me," Brodie said, over his shoulder. "The good float's on the right, and I'm here for a good float." He dug hard into the river, and Kyson watched the delta slide by as he backwatered. Then the left leg disappeared behind the grading landscape.

They rode the river, the dark water like gator scales in the sun. Then, the river constricted into a gorge and sped up in a loud hiss and burst. A gauntlet of boulders and banks, rushes and falls.

"Jesus," Kyson said, and, not looking back, Brodie yelled, "This is hair rafting, baby!"

They hit the chute and the g-force slid them up the right side of the S, then glided down and rode up the other side as the bend torsioned back. They stroked through a labyrinth of bony rapids that wrenched in a fall, and exploded through a curler, where the canoe boofed off the crest, spilling them. When they resurfaced, the boat was overturned and twisting in the wash, the gear and oars bobbing in the flat-water ahead.

Brodie threw his hands up and yelled, "That's what I'm talking about!"

"Sank in the drank," Kyson said, side-stroking toward the boat. He reached it and Brodie retrieved the gear.

They found a cavern at the foot of the cliff and swam to it. Got out and righted the boat, threw everything inside. A tongue of water curtained off the ceiling, and the river seen through it looked melted in molten glass. They climbed a large plate of limestone tectonic-ed against an end of the overhang, and dove and back-flipped from its pinnacle. Dubbed it "Memorial Rock" and, across its face, Brodie etched "MEMO" with the tactical knife and they toasted it, then boarded the canoe and shoved off. Watched "MEMO" disappear behind them.

Brodie smiled at Kyson.

"What?"

His smiled widened. "Fun, wasn't it?"

"Damn straight," Kyson said.

Brodie dug them forward, back muscles rolling under the skin. The letters of his tattoo morphing: U.s.M.c.

Kyson's oar bit in harmony. They were here and they were now, and Brodie was right. It was fun.

SEVERAL MILES DOWN, they skirted a vein.

"Somebody needs art lessons," Brodie said.

Covering the cliff facing, a painting of a green stick figure, hands bound above its head. Five red figures surrounding it.

"How you get up there to paint that?" Kyson said.

"With a clinched asshole."

Kyson watched it pass behind them, out of sight.

Farther down, they saw a second image—the green figure gutted, red spraying from the bowels. Roped entrails held above the red figures' heads.

"The hell?" Kyson said.

Brodie stood in the canoe and scanned above. Shielding his eyes, he looked where they'd come from. Studied where they were headed. "Keep going," he said, and sat.

They rounded again and stopped at the same time. The canyon walls on both sides were blood red. Top to water, as far as they could see.

"The hell is this?" Kyson said.

Brodie didn't answer. He plowed the oar in hard, and Kyson followed. They fought through a network of rapids, and Kyson's headache returned, his lung lining seared. His strokes began to slap off the water, and he stopped. "Hold on," he said, and spat.

"Don't stop," Brodie said.

"I need a minute," Kyson said, wrists draped over his knees.

Several more strokes and Brodie yanked his oar out. Glazed in sweat, he inhaled a single breath and heaved it out.

They drifted in circles but let it go.

"Hear that?"

Brodie tilted his head.

The canoe whirled and the buzzing deepened, like the audible oscillation of a power line hum.

"Yellow jacket nest," Brodie said.

"No," Kyson said, and pointed.

In the shade, lapping against the soggy bank was a dark mound in a swarming cloud.

They nosed toward it. Closer, they saw it was bloated at one end, the color of veins under pale skin. It was slick and coated with bluebottle flies.

Kyson put his face in the crook of his arm. Flies swarmed and landed on his head and ears and he swatted.

They scuttled over Brodie's face, circling off when he shook his head. He reached his oar out and pushed, and there was a release of gas as it rolled, and the fly cloud exploded.

Kyson leaned over and coughed.

It was half a human torso, split with precision up the sternum. The skull and a piece of the mandible attached and dangling, the soft tissue maggot-eaten away.

Brodie back-stroked, his lips tight. Tenting his shirt over his nose, Kyson spun them downriver and clawed forward.

"God," Kyson said, face bloodless. "We swam in that shit, man." He put a palm over his mouth. "I drank out of it."

"Just bury your paddle and keep going."

They rounded the next elbow and froze. Flanked along the right cliff top, not moving, were five nude figures holding what looked like handmade longbows. Their bodies the color of skinned muscle. The color of the cliffs.

"Brodie?" Kyson said.

"Don't," he whispered, "look." He knifed the blade of the oar into the water, barely slicing the surface. Extracted it just as easy.

Ahead, the muffled roar of rapids.

Kyson kept his paddle submerged, propelling with J-strokes, and in the mirrored ripples, he saw each figure draw its bow down in unison, and a scream erupted from the cliff top, so loud the air shimmied, the sound waves warbling the surface of the water. Droning moans ricocheted from cliff-to-cliff down the river.

He was reaching to cover his ears when Brodie was knocked off his seat as if yanked by a pulley. An arrow stemmed from his right side, the fletching of red feathers fluttering. His eyes wide, mouth open.

Kyson jumped toward him but his leg tethered. He looked down and an arrow had lodged in the meat of his thigh and stuck in the hull of the canoe. He wrapped a hand around each side of his quad and threw his head back, but his yell was drowned out by another scream above.

Arrows popped the side, punctured the cooler, strings of water tailing out. More flumped the surface around them and sank, yellow and refracted, in slow motion.

"Shit!" Kyson said, and felt a slap to the side of his head. He reached up, smeared two fingertips of blood from a gash.

The rapids were closer. He tugged the arrow pinning him and saw it was shafted in some sort of long bone, feathered from a cardinal wing. A broad head sculpted from a shard of toothed jawbone biting into the wood. He gripped low where the head was buried and lifted in a twist, so hard a crown popped loose.

A dark wave of arrows funneled down.

Brodie gurgled. He was hit through the bicep and hand, his knee and groin.

Kyson torqued harder and the shaft squealed and snapped, and he bellied over the side for cover. The boil jerked the rod and, reaching to remove it, his feet buoyed out the other side of the boat. There was a snap in his ankle, and this one he felt full force. Dragging it back, he saw the blood like black smoke underwater. The arrow sunk to the feathers.

They were entering the runnel, and the figures lowered their bows in unison.

Brodie twitched on the canoe bottom, and Kyson thought of the trout.

"Hang on!" Kyson said, and the rapids took them. A submerged boulder rocked against his floating ribs, spun him in the undertow. The arrows through his limbs poled into the riverbed and vaulted him, and he almost let go.

They rode a wave, and Kyson saw a hole in Brodie's cheek with a single band of flesh stretched thin and tacked to the bottom. They troughed and Kyson lost grip and went under. Resurfaced, and the flow smoothed out.

He looked above and the figures were gone. The screams had stopped.

He vomited river foam. "They're gone," he said, whipping his head around.

"God," Brodie said, and coughed a string of blood. "They won't want me now."

Kyson tightened his grip, still watching above.

"They won't want me now."

"Who won't?"

Brodie's eyes were cut toward Kyson. His jaw locked in a grimace.

"Of course they'll want you," Kyson said, and could see Brodie's back teeth through his cheek. "They need people like you."

Around the bend, the rush of another chute.

"They want survivors," Kyson said. He looked around for a bank, an overhang. Anything. "You're a survivor. A real American hero," he said. "And they don't die."

Inside the canoe, the leak-water had crimsoned. The thwarts were splintered. The bottom and port side quilled with arrows. Kyson's tilley hat floated by and wedged in a bush, and he thought about the drunk at Mason's, a life changer, he'd said, and that old bastard yelling, "I told 'em!" and his face cinched in a cry but he did not.

"They won't," Brodie said, glassy-eyed.

The rapids louder, the water faster. A fallen tree tremored as if shaken by invisible hands. They were entering the cut.

"Know what?" Kyson said. "We get out of here, I'll join with you. Buddy system, how's that?" Hooking his elbow over the side, he tried to straighten the yaw with his other hand. "'Cause they can hit us, goddamn it, but they can't kill us," he said, voice raised. "Semper fi!" he yelled, throwing his head back. "Oorah!"

Brodie said, "Oorah," in a blood-drowned voice.

"Semper fi!" Kyson yelled.

They rounded.

Brodie rolled his eyes from Kyson to the clouds above. "Oorah," he whispered, and a tear slid over his bloodied cheekbone and pearled down pink.

"Semper fi, baby!" Kyson said, flipping a middle finger to the world.

And above them, flanked along the left cliff top, not moving, were five nude figures. Bodies the color of skinned muscle. Longbows drawn as a scream pierced the land.

"Oorah," Kyson said, with what little breath he could.

Loyalty

ANATOLY BELILOVSKY

The author was born in a city that changed owners six or seven times in the last century, the latest crude attempt at adverse possession being in progress even as we speak. He was traded to the United States for a truckload of wheat, learned English from *Star Trek* reruns, and went on to become a Science Fiction & Fantasy Writers Association member in spite of chronic cat deficiency by publishing nearly one hundred pieces of original and translated prose and poetry.

THERE WAS SOME SERIOUS pucker factor on this mission. Grinch the pilot had all of five hours flight time in Kamov helicopters, we were wearing bogus insignia and squawking IFF codes bought off a corrupt officer, and I was thinking about my brother.

And then the radar warning beeped.

"Five minutes. Check your kit," Stanislavsky said. Not his real name, of course; all of us went by noms de guerre. All of us had families to think of.

By force of habit, all of us reached for the weapons first. Clean, loaded, safe. Not that they'd help us if things went to shit. Three men, four if you count the pilot, against a battalion? We looked at each other next. Two worn uniforms, one new. Stanislavsky's, of course, in command for this mission by virtue of his special training. You gonna play sub-colonel, you gotta dress sub-colonel. White duct tape on sleeves, in place of usual blue. One pair of Timberland boots, two of Chinese knockoffs. Three scowls under Balaklava masks.

Everyone expects the Russian Inquisition!

Circling for the landing. Two privates run out to the helipad, shielding their eyes against the rising sun; a sergeant walks more slowly from the Buk ground-to-air control bunker. The Alligator is painted in Navy blue and white, but that does not matter: GRU covers all the services.

The skids touch the dust, rotors slow down. We jump out, take our bearings, and turn to the privates.

"Battle alarm!" I yell. "Battalion muster, now!"

We watch the battalion assemble. The Major marches toward us, his deputy by his side.

"345th Battalion of 201st Motorized Division assembled and ready!"

"I have my doubts about that," Stanislavsky says, letting the long Os and the breathy Gs back into his voice.

Now the Major flinches. Stanislavsky code-switches back to the broad As of Moscow pronunciation. "Major, you are under arrest," he says and turns to the deputy. "Captain, detail four men to escort my soldiers and the Major to his quarters. He has ten thousand Euros to return to us."

It is now the Captain's turn to flinch. "It will be done, Sub-colonel." He gestures at a sergeant who taps three more men. The group departs, my men guarding the prisoner, battalion men guarding them all.

"Captain, your Major sold the IFF codes for the next week," Stanislavsky says. "They have been changed. Here are new ones." He hands a sheet of paper to the Captain. "Anything flies through your sector with old codes"—he points to the Buk launcher—"Any questions?"

"None."

"Good," Stanislavsky says. "Oh, one more thing."

"Yes?"

"General Tomsky, at headquarters?"

"Yes?"

"Today is not a good day to bother him reporting this. My own report left him in . . . quite the state."

"I understand."

The detail returns, empty handed. Everyone eyes each other. My men pretend not to notice.

"Nothing?" Stanislavsky says.

"Nothing, Sub-colonel," one of the men, a corporal, answers.

"Well, it's here somewhere. Find it."

"It will be done," the captain says. I have no doubt they'll try. And try. And try.

We climb on board. Before we close the hatch, the Captain salutes.

"Your boss is a fool," Stanislavsky says.

"I'll do better," the Captain says.

"I'm counting on it."

The rotor noise rises, and a moment later, the helicopter does too, swings wide around the Buk—control trailer, search radar, targeting radar, launcher, missile store—then we fly south toward the sea.

"You know I'm innocent, Sub-colonel," the Major says.

Stanislavsky says nothing. I'm thinking about the orders we intercepted. An attack on a fortified position. A suicide mission for his battalion, set for tomorrow.

We turn over the sea, the rising sun shining through the tail hatch. The pucker factor dissipates, slowly.

"Why are we headed west?" The Major asks. We let him work it out in silence. "Oh. You really are Ukrainian. I didn't know who you were when you offered me the money, Ukrainian Intelligence or Russian provocateurs. It didn't matter. I'm an honest soldier."

"I know, brother," I say, and pull my balaklava off my face.

The Major pales. "It's you!"

I nod. "Family black sheep at your service."

"Why?"

He has twenty centimeters of height and twelve kilos of muscle on me, always did, as we grew up in that gray zone just east of the Donets river. Always the bigger, tougher kid. Always able to take care of himself. Perhaps that's why he does not understand why anyone would want to join the underdog.

"Because you are my brother and I love you," I say. Because the underdog has teeth that would have torn you to shreds had I left you in place is the knowledge I keep to myself, for now, need-to-know.

He sighs. "So now what?"

"You ever read the Geneva Convention?"

"No. Have you?"

"Of course." I hand him a copy. "You'll love our POW camps."

He thinks I'm making fun of him. I'm not. He'll get a roof over his head, a bed, three squares, and a very sympathetic interrogator. He'll live.

Review: *Darkside*, by Michael Mammay

Nathan W. Toronto

Michael Mammay is a science fiction writer and a retired army officer. He is a graduate of the United States Military Academy and is a veteran of more wars than he cares to count. His novels include the *Planetside* series, *The Misfit Soldier*, and *The Weight of Command*. His next novel, *Darkside*, is out in September 2024. *Planetside* was named to Library Journal's best books of 2018 list, and the audiobook, narrated by R. C. Bray, was nominated for an Audie award for best science fiction audiobook. Michael lives with his wife in Georgia.

JUST WHEN WE THINK that Carl Butler can't possibly come out of retirement yet again, Michael Mammay finds a way to wow us once more. I was skeptical that Mammay could pull it off, that he could find some new way to keep it interesting, but his story about an old retired colonel investigating the death of a young girl's father tells us so much about the meaning of service and selfless leadership.

In spite of his gruff and cantankerous exterior, Carl Butler has a soft, chewy middle. He knows perfectly well when he's being a grade-A, premium douchebag, but he also knows when to do the right thing. And also what the right thing actually is. This is true even when it might cost him dearly. In fact, Butler's penchant for putting himself in harm's way, knowing the risks, is his most endearing quality, aside from his wry sense of humor.

Butler also has a penchant for attracting big-stakes problems, which is what makes *Darkside* refreshing, even though it's the fourth installment in the series. A young girl finds him one day, asking him to solve her father's murder. He doesn't feel up to it—he's really retired this time—but Butler's soft, chewy middle eventually carries the day and he gets in way, way over his head.

And getting in over his head puts a lot of other people in danger, including Mac, his right-hand man, and Ganos, his tech guru. That's when Butler's soft, chewy interior gives in to his gruff, cantankerous exterior and the story really gets moving.

Butler fights a bevy of enemies on behalf of others, but his frailties and foibles are always clear to the reader, which makes him so relatable and so easy to invest in. The reader knows that Butler will get out of the monstrous pickle he's put himself in, but Mammay's skill lies in hiding exactly how that will happen until the very last moment. This novel is a detective thriller wrapped in a glorious military science fiction story about understanding what goes through the mind of an old, surly colonel when he doesn't get what he wants and innocent, defenseless people are depending on him to succeed.

The story has flaws, but not many. Mammay never bills Butler as a superhero, but the way he takes a licking and keeps on ticking verges on superhuman. I chalk that up either to really good medical technology or to Mammay knowing a whole lot more than me about getting shot.

The series also feels a bit like it *may* have run its course. Just how many more times can Butler throw down with two big, nasty corporations before their depth of resources catches up with him? Sure, Butler is fabulously wealthy, but suspicion lurks that these corporations just might want to off him when he least expects, in spite of the compulsive measures that Butler and Mac take to protect him. In fact, the only way to really turn Butler's murder mystery stories on their end is to have Butler solve his own murder.

But who am I to suggest this to Mammay? *Darkside* earns five bullets from me. I thought this series was dead after three books, but Mammay found a way to surprise and thrill me with *Darkside*. I would happily be surprised again, and when Mammay writes another military science fiction book, I'll be sure to read it.

Also from BULLET POINT PRESS

SAGA OF THE EMERALD MOON
Nathan W. Toronto

Rise of Ahrik

Revenge of the Emerald Moon

Redemption of the White Planet
(coming soon)

BULLET POINTS
Nathan W. Toronto, ed.

Volumes 1–6

Subscribe to *Bullet Points*